This very lovely book belongs
to me and my name is:

LiLY

LavagnA

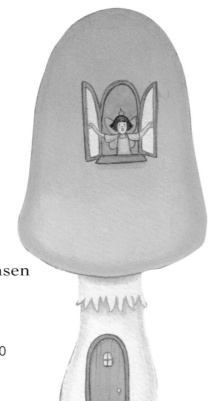

Illustrated by Natalie Hinrichsen
Cover art by Jacqueline East
Written by Mandy Archer

This edition published by Parragon in 2010

Parragon
Queen Street House
4 Queen Street
Bath BA1 1HE, UK

ISBN 978-1-4075-5518-8

Manufactured in China

Please retain this information for future reference.

Fairy

Daisy and the Secret Promise

PaRRagon

Bath · New York · Singapore · Hong Kong · Cologne · Delhi · Melbourne

A secret kingdom of fairy folk live among the roses at the bottom of Jessica Scott's back garden. Although Jessica plays there every day, she hasn't once seen the fairies.

She has never even glimpsed Daisy Dewdrop, a tiny fairy girl who is six, just like her.

Daisy and her friends love to peek at Jessica. But if she gets
too close, they quickly flutter away. Every young fairy knows that
fairies must stay hidden from humans.

One day, Daisy Dewdrop was helping to fairy-sit her three baby brothers, Fidget, Freckles and Fast-Toes.

"Watch this!" cried Daisy, gently tapping Freckles on the head with her wand.

Fidget and Fast-Toes giggled as Freckles turned green, then blue, then red.

"My turn,
my turn!"
the elvelets laughed,
tumbling in and out of
the blades of grass.

"All right," said Daisy, tiptoeing
after them. "But please sit still first!"

Fidget, Freckles and Fast-Toes did not want to sit still. Daisy tried all kinds of spells to keep her brothers amused, but nothing worked.

Suddenly, the fairy triplets grinned. "Let's play hide-and-seek!"

"Oh no, you don't!" glared Daisy, stamping her foot.

She raised her wand to cast a fairy freezing spell, but somehow the magic missed. Fairy dust was scattered far across the lawn, where Jessica lay colouring on a rug. The little girl found herself being showered in golden sparks.

Daisy Dewdrop gasped to see the girl freeze, but her magic was only strong enough to last an instant. Jessica shook her head and blinked, then scrambled over to find out what had happened.

"Quick, hide!" whispered Daisy,
chasing her brothers back to the roses.

Fairies all over the yard fluttered back to their houses.
Daisy gulped – she had broken the biggest rule in fairyland.

Jessica was now sure there were fairies in her yard and was determined to find them. She searched for them every day. "I know they're real," she told her mum at bedtime.

Before going to sleep, Jessica would gaze out of her bedroom window, longing for one more glimpse.

Down at the bottom of the garden, Daisy watched Jessica's light go out. This was the only time that it was safe for the fairies to flutter onto the lawn.

Daisy Dewdrop was sent to see the Fairy Queen.

"Your bad temper has put the whole kingdom in danger," said the Queen, frowning. "Now we have to hide ourselves away until after sunset. I will take your wand away until you can be trusted with it."

The young fairy sadly placed her star-topped wand in the Queen's lap.

Being a fairy who can't cast spells was no fun at all. While her friends used their wands to make rainbows and get their tiaras glittering, Daisy Dewdrop hid herself away among the rosebuds.

Suddenly, the rose Daisy was perched on began to wobble.
She saw Jessica above her, staring into the flowers.
"I wish the fairies would let me see them," sobbed Jessica.

Daisy pulled the rose petals around her until
the little girl walked away. She knew what it
was like to feel left out.

The next evening, all the young fairies polished their wands and gathered under the moonlight. There was going to be a royal magic competition and everyone was very excited. Daisy watched from her toadstool window, longing to take part.

At that moment, a line of fireflies appeared, lighting up the garden.

The Fairy Queen stepped out of the darkness,
the jewels in her crown shimmering like stars.
She looked beautiful.

"Good evening, Fairies, Elves and Sprites!" said the Fairy Queen. Her tiny subjects curtsied and waved their wands in a circle around their Queen.

All of a sudden, a
booming voice echoed
around the circle.

"I've found you!"
said the voice.

A giant pair of hands
came out of the skies and
lifted up the Fairy Queen!

Daisy Dewdrop gasped.

The air sparkled as frightened fairies fluttered into the shadows. Jessica was standing in the middle of the lawn, gently cradling the Fairy Queen in her hands.

"I knew I'd find you, even if I had to sneak out in my pyjamas!" said Jessica.

"Please let her go!" called Daisy. But Jessica couldn't hear her. To humans, fairy voices sound like bells *tinkling* in a breeze.

Daisy saw her **big** chance.

She **jumped** out of her toadstool house...

...then hovered up to Jessica's face.

Without her wand, all she could do was point to the poor Fairy Queen.

Somehow, Jessica seemed to understand. "Oh! I won't hurt her," she whispered. "I just wanted to make sure you were real."

Daisy unclipped a delicate chain from around her neck. Jessica looked in wonder at the tiny fairy. "For me? Thank you!"

Then something amazing happened. The necklace glittered and grew until it was just the right size for a girl to wear! Somehow Daisy's kind heart had made one last drop of fairy magic.

Jessica released the Fairy Queen at once.
"I won't tell anyone about you, I promise!" she said.

Daisy watched as Jessica ran home, clutching her fairy necklace and smiling at the thought of her secret promise.

As a reward for her bravery, the Fairy Queen presented Daisy Dewdrop with a very special gift – a brand-new, sparkling star-topped wand!